MESKWAKI AND THE PRESIDENT
A TALE OF A FOX AND HIS URGENT MISSION TO THE WHITE HOUSE

Written by Vivaldo Andrade dos Santos
Illustrations by Rafa Antón

MESKWAKI AND THE PRESIDENT

vivaldosantos10@gmail.com

Second Edition: May 2019
Printed in the United States of America
ISBN: 9781096460510

To Heather, Chimi, and Zuzu

CONTENTS

CHAPTER ONE: Mama Bear 1

CHAPTER TWO: The Council 3

CHAPTER THREE: The Foxes 7

CHAPTER FOUR: Meskwaki 12

CHAPTER FIVE: The Journey 16

CHAPTER SIX: At the National Zoo 20

CHAPTER SEVEN: Heading to the White House 23

CHAPTER EIGHT: Arriving at the White House 26

CHAPTER NINE: At Play in the First Lady's Garden 29

CHAPTER TEN: The Secret Service Plan .36

CHAPTER ELEVEN: The Media 38

CHAPTER TWELVE: Meskwaki Meets the President 40

CHAPTER THIRTEEN: In the White House Press Room 44

CHAPTER FOURTEEN: Meskwaki Says Goodbye to Washington 46

CHAPTER FIFTEEN: Back in the Forest 49

CHAPTER ONE

MAMA BEAR

ON A FINE AFTERNOON, somewhere in the Appalachian forest, Mama Bear summoned all the animals to an assembly.

Mr. Redheaded Woodpecker was snacking on some grubs from an old tree when Mama Bear roared at him: "Hey, Redhead! Listen to me! I need you to tell all our friends to come here right now!"

The request surprised Mr. Redheaded Woodpecker. But before he could say anything, Mama Bear continued, "I don't have time to go knocking on everyone's door. Go on your speedy wings and spread the word."

"What am I supposed to tell them?"

"Tell them I am going to meet the President of the United States."

Mr. Redheaded Woodpecker cocked his head.

"Hurry now. Seeing the President is urgent business."

MAMA BEAR had awoken that morning grouchier than usual. She was known for being headstrong. She roared, and when she was especially upset, Mama Bear smelled fierce.

Mr. Redheaded Woodpecker could tell Mama Bear was determined, so he listened and followed her orders. He dashed off to spread the word to all the animals to come listen to Mama Bear, with help from his buddies: the flycatchers, thrushes, wrens, hawks, nuthatches, sapsuckers, and warblers.

An hour later, all the animals were gathered to listen to Mama Bear.

All but the Fox family.

It must be said that in the Law of the Forest, when such meetings were called by one of its inhabitants, the natural course of life was suspended and a truce took place. In this way, despite some feelings of suspicion and a bit of fear, Ms. Hare, Mr. Rabbit, and Chipmunk Jr., to name a few, were just fine hanging out with Mr. Bobcat, who nevertheless couldn't resist licking his lips and dreaming about his dinner later that evening. Both Mr. Frog and Mrs. Grouse would jump every time Mrs. Rattlesnake shook her rattle.

However, not all the animals were happy to get up in the middle of their afternoon naps to attend a meeting. Ms. Bat, Mrs. Great Horned Owl, and Mr. Screech Owl kept yawning and rubbing their crusty eyes to stay awake.

"What on Earth could Mama Bear want now?" They wondered.

After all, it was not even dusk, and they all had plans for that evening.

CHAPTER TWO
THE COUNCIL

MAMA BEAR STOOD UP on the trunk of a dead tree.

"First of all," she began, "I want to thank you all for coming to this meeting. I called you together because I am going to meet the President of the United States. He is the only person who can resolve any problems, and this president has a reputation for listening to everyone."

The animals looked at each other. Knowing how Mama Bear could be fierce, they didn't say a word.

"You all know Bernie Bear, don't you? Bernie is my beloved nephew and godson. My sister just told me the sad news about him leaving the forest with his friend to find food in the nearby city. He came back home with a broken paw. His friend never came back. Bernie is very distressed."

Mama Bear recounted this story with a sad tone in her voice.

"Because of that, now Junior, my toddler, can't play with Bernie until poor Bernie's paw gets better! Besides his injury, Bernie came home very smelly from scavenging in garbage bins in the city. No mother can put up with stinky kids!"

Mama Bear fell silent.

Then she said urgently, "We need the President's help. We are hungry!"

"Yes, someone needs to talk to Mr. President," Mr. Bobcat said.

"Hooray!" The other animals shouted.

Mr. Raccoon had ignored what Mama Bear said. After all, the other animals made fun of him because his relatives had long ago moved to the cities. He never envied his city-dwelling cousins. In fact, he felt proud of his forest life because most of his urban cousins had never seen a real fish.

"How gross it is to lick sardine and tuna-fish cans found in garbage bins! *Yuck!* I have no rotten teeth because I don't eat leftover donuts, cupcakes, and muffins! And to think of Halloween! Disgusting! All those peanut-butter cups and chocolate candy. *Ick!* I never got a bellyache because I don't eat all that revolting stuff!" Mr. Raccoon mused to himself.

Flying Squirrel Jr. and his friends became so excited about the whole topic that they jumped and flew around.

Truth be told, the Squirrel family found everything exciting.

Yet, they also had their own concern: "We demand our tall trees back so we can practice for our yearly flying competition," they cried.

"I second that," said Mr. Redheaded Woodpecker, in an exultant voice: "If there are no trees, what are we supposed to peck on?"

Ms. Chattahoochee Slimy Salamander spoke up too: "Day after day the Snapping Turtle family is getting moodier and moodier," she said.

"Hold your horses," Turtle Jr. snapped.

"The muddy bottoms of the rivers where we spend most of our time are covered with glass and plastic bottles. Our skin is turning black."

Mrs. Turtle added, "We can't breathe under water with all the waste dumped in the water. I can't find places to lay my eggs."

Mr. Skunk spoke up. "Our spray used to be nastier than greasy onion smell. No longer, because our diet has changed. And, why in the world do the humans use our beautiful fur coats to make jackets for themselves?"

Mrs. Porcupine also spoke up, interrupting Mr. Skunk. On that day she had horrible allergies, and as she spoke, all the animals feared she would sneeze.

What if she sent one of her sharp quills flying? Mr. Fisher shuddered recalling how long it took him to remove all those painful quills from his face from an altercation he had with Mrs. Porcupine. It was hellish! How everyone laughed at that fight between tiny Mr. Fisher and giant Porcupine!

Mrs. Great Horned Owl got everyone's attention with a great hoot. "It's going to grow dark soon," she said. "We have so many complaints, we could go on talking until tomorrow!"

All the animals agreed, and a loud *bravissimo* of roars, screeches, tweets, squeaks and squeals, gobblings, hissings, snappings, and croaking filled the forest.

Mrs. Great Horned Owl cried out again.

"We must see the President and ask for help, but I am not sure about Mama Bear going…"

"What do you mean?" Mama Bear cocked her head.

"Let me make my point," Mrs. Great Horned Owl continued.

Mrs. Great Horned Owl had a reputation of being very wise and respected, not only because of her knowledge, but also because of her glowing golden irises that had already started shining in the dark as the night was approaching and because of those brutal claws of hers, which were capable of tearing a prey apart.

"How are you going to meet the President without calling attention to yourself?"

"Who, if not Mama Bear, could do it? Who would?" The animals asked themselves.

"I propose we write a letter. Everyone of us sign it, and we have someone in the Foxes' family deliver it."

"The Foxes?"

There was a loud murmur of confusion in the crowd.

CHAPTER THREE
THE FOXES

THE FACT IS that the Foxes didn't show up for the meeting.

Besides being known for their cunning personalities, the Foxes had a reputation for never taking part in an assembly, such as the one taking place that afternoon.

The Foxes had their reason for skipping such a gathering.

The Foxes all knew the story of the trial of their great-great-great-great-great-grandfather — the greatest of them all — Reynard Fox.

Reynard Fox had been tried for tricking all the animals.

Since the Foxes did not have a trustworthy reputation, the animals were reluctant to send a fox to see the President.

Great debate ensued. Finally, Mrs. Great Horned Owl, concerned the meeting was approaching a deadlock, turned to Mama Bear.

"I'll get the Foxes," Mama Bear sighed.

With that, despite being a bit clumsy, Mama Bear headed to the nearest hole and put her mouth close to it.

She roared into the Foxes' home: "Hey, Foxes! We need to talk to you right now. Please, come out!"

Down in the burrow the Foxes were sleeping. At first, they didn't wake up. Mama Bear roared loudly, and her voice echoed from one hole to another, from gallery to gallery, from chamber to chamber, forcing the Foxes to hear what she had to say. Mama Bear's echoing voice awoke them, and soon the whole family was on guard, lifting their ears to hear what was being said. At this time Mama Bear's voice sounded like a solicitation, rather than like someone who was hungry or angry. However, Mama Bear's voice still couldn't persuade them to come out.

GROWING IMPATIENT and worried about nightfall, Mrs. Great Horned Owl screeched, "The Russians are coming! The Russians are coming!"

Everyone in the forest knew how the Russians had domesticated foxes, turning them to pets. Any mention of Russians was enough to get the Foxes' attention.

Mrs. Great Horned Owl knew about the Russian story. It was the only card she could play to get them out of their holes. The Foxes always feared the Russians. Some of the animals thought that it was a made up story and shrugged their shoulders. Yet, she had read about that somewhere in her *encyclOWLpedia*, and other people had written about it. Mrs. Great Horned Owl felt empathy for her clever neighbors, but she had no other choice. If she wanted the Foxes to join the general meeting, she felt she was left with no choice but to invoke "the Russian paranoia".

As soon they heard that the Russians were coming, the Foxes screeched, their ears twitched and pointed backwards.

The Foxes shuddered to think what could happen to them if the Russians, indeed, came.

"I don't want to be a dog!" One cried.

"I like my pricked-up ears," another squealed, while pulling his ears to see how they would feel being floppy. "Aren't floppy ears signs of laziness, Mom?"

Down in the foxhole there was much fretting about life as a dog, about being rubbed on the belly, and being made to fetch a ball. The idea of throwing them something to fetch seemed very silly. Don't get me wrong. The Foxes loved fetching, especially flying birds, jumping grasshoppers, running mice, quick salamanders. When food was brought home, there was no wagging the tail — that kind of thing — but lots of growling, scratching and swaying around since the food was never enough for all of them. It was a way to learn how to share food with each other as well a way to force them to go out and look for food themselves, if they felt they didn't get enough. "I can't imagine our kids greeting each other by sniffing each other's butt. *Yuck!*" Mrs. Foxes said.

Finally, Mr. Fox agreed to come out of their hole and see what the meeting was about.

"Alas, the Russians are coming..." he said.

As he walked out of their hole, Mr. Fox saw all the animals gathered, expecting him.

When Mama Bear greeted him, Mr. Fox said, "Wait, but where are the Russians?"

"Well," Mrs. Great Horned Owl said, "they haven't arrived yet, but they will eventually come. Yes, them. Or, others with similar intentions. Mama Bear called this meeting because someone needs to meet the President and discuss certain issues with him regarding life in the forest. And we all agreed that a Fox should do it. We decided to write a letter and have you deliver it."

"Me?" Mr. Fox asked.

Mrs. Great Horned Owl said, "Who has the reputation of being the most cunning among us?"

Mr. Fox smiled slyly. As he grinned, he retracted his sharp claws. The Foxes were proud of their special, retractable claws which were used to minimize any noise while walking, making the foxes excellent hunters, as skilled as their feline neighbors.

"Who, among us, could outfox Mr. President, if not one of the Foxes? He is a politician," Mrs. Great Horned Owl said. "In our *encyclOWLpedia* a politician is defined as a combination of the Bears and the Foxes. Someone that governs and seems to have a final word about the way things should be."

All the animals nodded. Mama Bear was not quite happy with the comparison, but she nodded in agreement with a frown on her face.

Mrs. Great Horned Owl continued, "However, a politician doesn't need to be as big or physically as strong as Mama Bear, but still has to make his or her roar to be heard, calling the shots. His or her size could be compensated by some of the talents that the Foxes have. Politicians are known for being cunning. Sly as a fox, some people would say."

Feeling full of pride, Mr. Fox said, "I don't think I can do it. I am a bit too old for long journeys. Besides, my dearest wife and I are still nurturing some of the kids. However, I will have a private *wow wow wow* with my wife."

BACK DOWN IN the foxhole, Mr. and Mrs. Fox debated the situation.

Finally, Mrs. Fox sighed and suggested, "How about Meskwaki, darling?"

CHAPTER FOUR

MESKWAKI

MESKWAKI was the Foxes' eldest son. He got his name from his godfather who had traveled from territory to territory. The color of his beautiful orangish-red fur reminded his godfather of the *Meskwaki* people from the forest in the north who believed they were created out of red clay.

Every time his parents taught the little foxes techniques for digging, Meskwaki was the first among his siblings to start digging, and he always loved rolling on the dry red clay, especially when the sun was hot. However, after playing in the dirt, it was common to see Meskwaki compulsively chewing, scratching, and licking himself while trying to take a nap.

"I know the dirt makes your skin feel good, sweetie, but rolling in the dirt wakes up all the fleas and ticks who love to suck your sweet blood," his mother explained to him.

"*Grrr...grrr... grrr...* Bloodsuckers!"

It was very common to see Meskwaki roaring in his sleep, as if he were dreaming about fights with his siblings or hunting adventures. Sometimes he

dreamed he was lost in the forest and couldn't find his parents. His mother tried to minimize his stress by bringing him close to her body, licking his neck and eyes with affection, letting him know that it was just a bad dream and that everything was fine. Then he would continue sleeping, peacefully, until hunger would wake him up.

Meskwaki was not too much older than his brothers and sisters, but he had already learned how to dig and how to smell the wind to spot danger and food. His parents taught him the art of killing, and he knew from the Law of the Forest to only kill for food, or when life was at risk. Since he learned to eat pretty much anything, especially vegetables and fruits, killing was not always urgent. Besides, if he craved some meat, Meskwaki always found some tasty carrion to enjoy. Despite all this teaching, very important for his survival, his parents also taught him how to spot a prey, how to pounce on top of it, how to pin it down, and how to use his piercing canines on his prey's neck, if needed.

Meskwaki was a great student. He put all those techniques into practice, pouncing on grasshoppers, crickets, beetles, earthworms, and mice that he found. He also learned how to mark his territory with his own pee and follow his trail to get back home.

The fact that Meskwaki was going through his *foxlescence* helped Mr. and Mrs. Fox to make their decision about who to send to Washington, DC. Traditionally, it was during the *foxlescence* that the oldest fox would go on a personal journey. Mr. Fox used to brag about going as far as 40 miles away from home when he was Meskwaki's age. It was a very common thing among the boys. Learning how to survive in the forest was not the purpose of this particular trip, but it could serve him very well to learn something new.

The Foxes told Meskwaki and his siblings about this very special journey, this very special mission. His brothers and sisters would miss him, but it was time for Meskwaki to go.

Meskwaki, however, had mixed feelings about his parents' decision. He thought of himself as brave and felt proud to be chosen, but he was also afraid. He was excited by the adventure but wondered how it would be sleeping alone at night and hunting by himself. Would bigger animals, unaware of the Law of the Forest, attack him? What if he couldn't find food? Would he be scared of the people and unfamiliar things in the city? Would he miss his parents and his siblings, the comfort of his home?

MESKWAKI and his parents climbed out of their foxhole, joined the large gathering of animals, and announced their decision. There were many cheers again.

Meskwaki approached Mama Bear and Mrs. Great Horned Owl, who still stood at the center of the gathering.

"Where does the President live?" Meskwaki asked.

Mrs. Great Horned Owl noticed his apprehension. She consulted her *encyclOWLpedia* and told Meskwaki that the President lived in the city of Washington, in the District of Columbia (aka DC) precisely at 1600 Pennsylvania Avenue NW, in a big house called the White House. She warned him about the mice and rats from the cities being not as good to eat as the ones in the forest, and then she added, "Watch out for the birds. Most of them are starlings, pigeons, robins, sparrows, and those annoying mocking birds that will taunt you to death. I am not sure if you would like to snack on them if you knew what they eat."

"What other animals live in the city besides rats? Where do they sleep? Are there any trees to make shelter?" Meskwaki kept asking questions.

"Near DC there is a large river full of geese." Mrs. Great Horned Owl added.

But there were too many questions that she couldn't answer, and the *encyclOWLpedia* she had was not the updated edition.

Mr. Raccoon stepped in and started telling Meskwaki what he had learned from his relatives who lived in cities.

Mrs. Rabbit and Flying Squirrel Jr. and his cousins made Meskwaki promise to obey the Law of the Forest and not chase their relatives. At first Meskwaki rolled his eyes, but then he agreed. Meskwaki told them he would eat only berries and carrion while traveling.

Mama Bear and the other animals were getting tired and hungry. Noticing the growing agitation in the crowd, Mrs. Great Horned Owl quickly drafted a letter with all the issues the residents of the forest had. She was the only one among them who knew how to read and write. Mrs. Fox, with the help of Mr. Raccoon who had very skilled hands, made a pouch to be placed on Meskwaki's neck with the letter inside.

Mrs. Great Horned Owl asked, "Do I hear a motion to adjourn?"

All the animals were already leaving, and there was no time for the motion to be seconded.

Mrs. Fox strapped the pouch with the letter around Meskwaki's neck. Meskwaki said good-bye to his family, Mama Bear, and Mrs. Great Horned Owl and headed to Washington, DC.

CHAPTER FIVE
THE JOURNEY

THE FOREST was not too far away from Washington, DC, but still it would take Meskwaki a few days to get there. The closer he got to the city, the more he noticed how the animals were becoming scarce. He also noticed fewer and fewer trees. The high sun and the moon shone through the top of the sparse trees. He didn't dislike the dry leaves on the ground. He rolled in them to scratch his back, and that is when he noticed there were no salamanders around.

The "Manders" lived in the mushy areas, protected from the sunlight by the trees. Meskwaki loved to snack on them when he was hungry. Other times, he just liked poking them for fun, chasing them and putting his paws on top of them to make them struggle before letting them go. The Manders never liked being played with by a fox. But they were Manders and Meskwaki was a fox, after all. And that was part of life in the forest. Meskwaki missed the animals there.

Meskwaki trotted through the thinning forest for two days before stopping at a mountaintop where he could see DC in the distance. The city still appeared far away, but he didn't mind. When he grew tired, he found an abandoned hole to sleep in. When hungry, he had some berries and tasty grasshoppers for food. Grasshoppers were not part of the promise he made to his friends in the forest, so it was fine to munch on them. After a nap, he continued his journey.

At one point Meskwaki sniffed the air for a fine and delicious scent. The wind blew the smell of carrion towards him. He pointed his long nose towards where it was coming from.

However, the carrion was not the only smell in the air. Meskwaki's snout twitched more than usual.

"A distant relative?" He wondered.

He sniffed again. And that's when he noticed Mr. Gray Fox between him and the carrion.

Mr. Gray Fox was starving, so he went after the carrion.

As he did, Meskwaki leapt too. Suddenly, the two foxes were in a fight for food.

They stood on their hind legs, putting their front paws on each other's shoulders, pushing each other over. Then they both grabbed it with their sharp teeth. Each took a piece.

The sun was high and hot, and each of the foxes retreated to their own quiet, safe, shady bush to take a rest. They found bushes across from one another and napped. But the foxes slept with eyes semi-opened, always on guard, to ward off any potential attacks.

When Mr. Gray Fox woke up, he said to Meskwaki, "I've seen more and more red foxes in our territory these days."

Meskwaki knew about his relatives. His parents used to tell them many stories about Mr. Gray Fox's family. Meskwaki stared at him and said, "It is not by choice we have come here. We are being pushed out of our wooded forest. Now we have to share our space with humans."

Mr. Gray Fox listened.

"But, I am just passing by this time," Meskwaki said. "I am heading to Washington, DC to meet Mr. President."

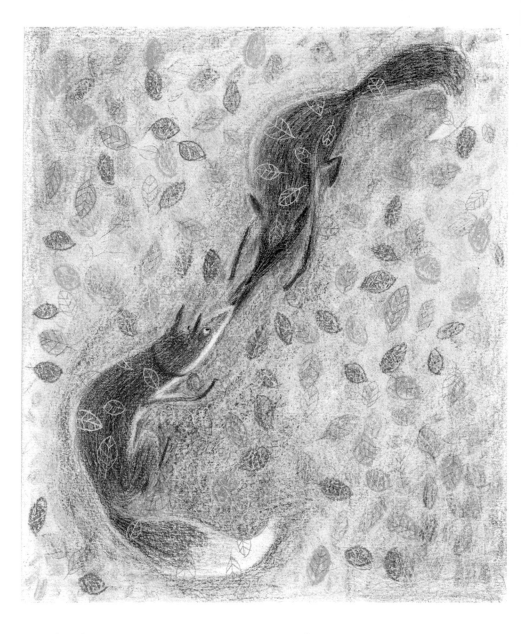

"What for?" Mr. Gray Fox was very surprised.

"I was chosen to deliver a letter from all my neighbors about the problems we have in the forest..."

Meskwaki pointed with his nose to the pouch strapped to his neck.

Mr. Gray Fox knew Meskwaki had an important mission and wished him good luck, then pointed him in the direction of the city and nodded goodbye.

AS MESKWAKI continued his journey, he learned from other animals more about the city, about who lived there and the danger of cars and the humans. He heard about the animals that people kept at home, especially dogs, hamsters, cats, geckos, iguanas, boas, cockatiels, and goldfish. All those tasty little creatures made his mouth water and his eyes widen with excitement.

But at first Meskwaki didn't learn anything new about the White House. After all, none of the animals he had met so far had ever been inside it. Eventually, he met a family of turkeys who told him what they knew from family stories. One of them had been inside the White House during a ceremony in which he was "pardoned" during something the humans called Thanksgiving. After that turkey was set free, he came back to the forest to tell the other turkeys about the giant white human house.

Meskwaki also came to learn that the President lived in the White House with his wife, their daughter, and their dog. He was curious to see the President's dog, although Meskwaki had not forgotten what his parents said about dogs and the Russians. The idea of being a pet came back to his mind and gave him the jitters. It was unconceivable for him to walk around with a leash on his neck or to *bow wow* through a window when seeing a squirrel or a bird through the glass and not being able to catch them. Those thoughts reminded him that his mission was urgent and he should keep going.

CHAPTER SIX

AT THE NATIONAL ZOO

MESKWAKI ARRIVED IN DC at night and decided to stop at the National Zoo.

As he snuck in, he didn't recognize some of the animals. He thought Mama Bear and Mr. Moose were the biggest, but what a surprise when he saw elephants and giraffes! He cried out when he saw lions, cheetahs, and tigers. The pandas made him think about Mama Bear, and the monkeys made him think about Flying Squirrel Jr, especially the way they loved climbing trees.

"Oh my! I would be in trouble if I messed with those animals. They seem healthy but they don't seem happy, panting and pacing in those cages. Why are they kept here?" Meskwaki wondered.

It made him miss his neighbors.

The Zoo's animals sensed the new visitor and stayed alert, especially the fennec foxes, a very tiny relative from the Sahara desert who had big ears and lived inside the Mammal House.

Meskwaki had amazing hearing so he could hear the animals' voicing their sense of distress as he wandered around the Zoo. Meskwaki heard them as they started talking to him:

"Hey, little friend. You shouldn't be here," Charlie, the fennec fox, said.

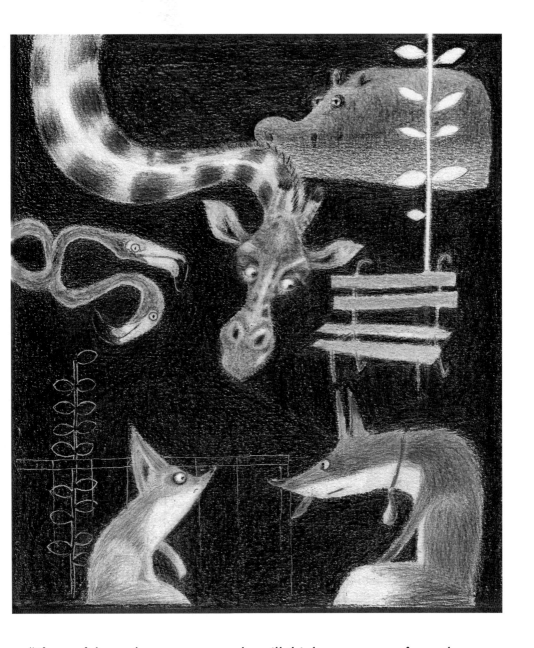

"If one of the zookeepers sees you, he will think you are one of us and you will be put in one of these cages," another animal said.

"How I miss running free in the forest and hanging out with my family and friends," another sighed with sadness.

Meskwaki started thinking about life in the forest and his family.

"What would happen to me if I was captured and put into a cage like these animals? I would never be able to see my family or run free again."

Meskwaki realized that most of the wild animals in the city, with the exception of pets, lived in the National Zoo.

The Zoo was a sad thing, Meskwaki thought. After all, nothing was more traumatic for a creature than being put in a cage, or in a fenced and walled simulation of a natural habitat. Meskwaki was glad he had made a stop at the Zoo to learn. Before he headed out to the White House, he said, "My dear friends, I will make sure to bring up the issue of your conditions in the Zoo when I meet Mr. President."

The animals wished him good luck. Then, Meskwaki headed to the White House through the Rock Creek Park. He hid in the shadow of the night, trotting silently along the Potomac River toward the National Mall, a vast green area where the White House and many monuments were located.

CHAPTER SEVEN
HEADING TO THE WHITE HOUSE

THE CITY was a strange place for Meskwaki.

The cars were aggressive, fast, and loud.

In the dark of night, Meskwaki was spotted by their headlights and ran into any bush he found. His ears were sensitive to city noises, and the honking drove him crazy. Tired, he fell asleep under some bushes in the Foggy Bottom neighborhood.

When the day broke, he woke up to piercing, alarming sounds of fire trucks and ambulances. The confusing noises of the city scared Meskwaki the most. More than ever, he missed his family and life in the forest, especially the singing of the birds, the chirping of crickets, and the running of the water in the creek.

Suddenly, his thoughts were interrupted by more and more honks. The noises intensified and became stranger as the traffic slowed to a stop, and the pedestrians stood still. Meskwaki watched. He realized that it was the President's motorcade passing by.

"But, how to get close to Mr. President?" Meskwaki wondered.

He stayed hidden from the people in the bushes. From there he could see

the convoy of many motorcycles, black vans, and identical black Cadillac
limousines, slowly passing one after another, along with men from the Secret
Service wearing black suits and sunglasses, discreetly talking on their ear piece
microphones. Meskwaki decided that this was not the time to approach the
President after all. Besides, he had no idea in which car the President would be.

If he wanted to talk to him, he would have to come up with a plan.

To meet the President at the White House seemed to be Meskwaki's only choice.

"But how will I get there without being noticed?" Meskwaki wondered.

Getting into the White House, a fenced residence with dozens of Secret Service agents guarding it, how could that be possible?

"Listen, Meskwaki…" He heard his mother's voice in his head telling him about the importance of his journey. That gave him renewed courage to carry on.

So, he stayed hidden until the motorcade passed, night arrived, and then he headed onto the National Mall.

All the information Mr. Gray Fox and the turkey family gave him before arriving in Washington, DC was coming in quite handy. Meskwaki passed by the Lincoln Memorial, and since there was nobody around that late in the night, climbed the stairway and wandered around the large statue of Lincoln. From there he looked straight ahead, just like any tourist visiting the city, and saw the Washington Monument and the U.S. Capitol Building behind it. Trotting with his little paws, he walked down the stairs of the monument. Then he walked calmly by the Reflecting Pool and turned left towards his final destination.

"The White House should be close," Meskwaki thought.

CHAPTER EIGHT
ARRIVING AT THE WHITE HOUSE

MESKWAKI APPROACHED the White House at dawn. He was surprised by how easy it was to get inside the property.

Or so it seemed.

He didn't see very many guards or secret service agents around. But unbeknownst to Meskwaki, there was a reason for that: the government was facing a shutdown. A shutdown happened when the Congress, the people who worked with the President, had a major disagreement with him, and reached a deadlock.

In the forest, with the exception of the ants, beavers, and the bees, who were really good at teamwork, most of the animals worked alone. A government shutdown was like if the worker bees stopped working. The whole beehive would be compromised, affecting the nectar production, the pollen gathering, and the brood.

The shutdown might have not been pleasant to many people, but it worked well for Meskwaki. Because of it, he was able to weasel his way into the White House with no difficulty, shimmying under the metal fence and into a bushy area. It was early morning, so he could slip in before a multitude of tourists packed in front of the residence to take pictures, hoping to see the President or his family... or at least their dog.

In his first hours in the city, Meskwaki learned how to stay away from people. There was always a fuss around the White House. DC was known for these things. The American people, since they were kids, learned about the city. To visit the capital was part of the experience of being American. Every day kids from all over the country walked around the National Mall and saw the monuments, the museums, the Capitol, the cherry blossoms, the pandas at the Zoo, and many other things, and, of course, they all took a photo in front of the White House.

The Secret Service seemed to be concerned, especially with the North Lawn where people gathered to take photos. This was because once in a while someone would leap the fence onto the residence lawn and make Jordan and Hurricane, the two dogs who guarded the White House, work. The presidential pet was too cute for tasks like that. But he got excited looking through the window, barking and wagging his tail when that kind of action took place on the grounds.

MESKWAKI STOOD as quietly as he could, peeking through the leaves, waiting for the right moment to explore the terrain and, eventually, to act. He avoided the East Entrance, where visitors entered the building, and found an easier way to approach the White House near a large garden full of rose bushes. He found his way around the fences, keeping himself deep in the bushes. He was so tired from his long journey that he soon fell asleep under a thick bush, where he stayed until night came.

It was dark when he decided to get closer to the White House. Meskwaki saw that only a few Secret Service agents were still around. However, he did not make himself too comfortable. After all, he was well aware of the dangers of entering a strange territory.

That was a lesson he had learned well from his parents.

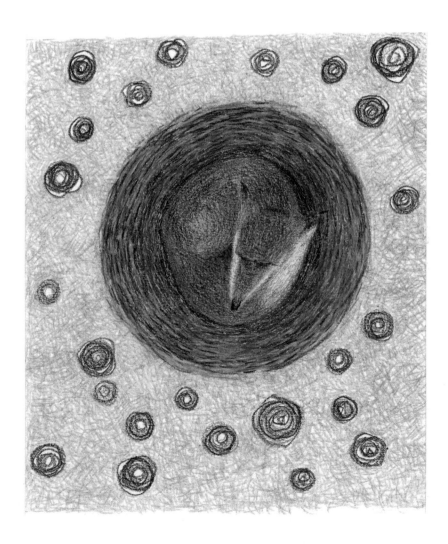

CHAPTER NINE

AT PLAY IN THE FIRST LADY'S GARDEN

THE WHITE HOUSE was surrounded with bushes, trees, and a beautiful trimmed lawn. It was too manicured for Meskwaki and his family's tastes. They preferred the wilderness, the rough and tumble of the forest, where they could put to use all their talents to hunt, their skill to escape when necessary, to play hide-and-seek or chase each other for fun.

Meskwaki found a new hiding place among the brambles. He noticed how soft the plot of soil was. This earth felt different from the forest floor, where he used to put his sharp retractable claws to good use. Since he was not sure how long it would take until he could meet the President, Meskwaki wisely decided to make himself a home in that garden full of rose bushes. The air smelled so fragrant there.

He started digging as fast as he could, and in a few hours, before morning came, he had dug a hole large enough to both sleep and hide in.

Resting in his new dwelling, Meskwaki decided that the letter would be delivered to the President when a good opportunity arose. Until then, he would settle into his fragrant new home and wait.

After all the digging, Meskwaki was exhausted once again. He slept, and when he woke up, it was already night. He was starving. Aside from some crickets, he found nothing else too exciting to eat. He carefully ventured beyond the garden of roses and came across a water fountain that reminded him of the creeks in the forest. He flicked his ears and sniffed the air to check for danger, and seeing no secret service personnel around, he decided to sip from the fountain. The water tasted different, but it was not so bad. He was thirsty, after all, and didn't think he should be picky.

When he looked around, Meskwaki spotted a garden of vegetables and fruits. Meskwaki's mouth watered.

"What a paradise! How happy Mr. Raccoon would be if had seen such a delight as this!" He thought!

Meskwaki munched on strawberries, tomatoes, and apples he found on the ground.

THE GARDEN was very quiet. What Meskwaki could not have known was that many of the grounds-crew had recently been furloughed during the government shutdown. But even though Meskwaki practically had the garden to himself he still needed to watch out for Mr. Haney.

Mr. Haney was a sweet old man who had been working as a grounds keeper at the White House for over 40 years and he definitely knew every corner of the lawn. Nevertheless, Mr. Haney would only be around if he had decided to take the President's dog for an evening walk.

Meskwaki darted across the grounds of the White House. Unfortunately, as he did, he triggered the motion sensors around the residence, causing a commotion and waking everybody up. Alarms went off, all the lights in the White House

went on, and the presidential dog woke up the entire family of the President.

Suddenly, several Secret Service agents, men and women, swarmed the grounds and talked on their ear piece headphones. Jordan and Hurricane raced, free of their muzzles. They barked loudly.

MESKWAKI had no idea where all these creatures came from.

When Meskwaki saw the lights on, he dashed back to the Rose Garden to his burrow in the ground where he felt secure.

Meskwaki dug down and kept digging in one direction for a long time, only changing directions once in a while to avoid all the underground pipes and roots. But every time he changed directions, he ended up scratching something harder than tree roots. He even tried to use his semi-retractable claws, but he realized that his claws were useless; he was up against solid concrete. Meskwaki, it seemed, had reached the White House bunker, a secret place where the President could be taken in case it was necessary.

No matter how persistent Meskwaki was, he could never dig through the bunker. He remembered his grandfather, the one who named him "Meskwaki," mentioning how hard it was to dig through a termite mound. A "termite mound" — that was the only thing Meskwaki could think about to compare this with. The tunnel was getting longer and longer, and despite the fact that Meskwaki had good eyes to see in the dark and skilled claws, he was getting tired of digging. He dug so much that if it were possible to take an X-ray of the White House grounds, one could see a long tunnel going in all different directions.

"If my family was with me here, we would dig together as we used to do in the forest where we built our home," Meskwaki thought. He sighed in exhaustion.

Hours passed. Meskwaki slept, and when he awoke it was by the growling of his stomach. Once again he decided to change direction in digging, this time away from the bunker. Then, after some time digging, he felt the grounds soften, grow more moist, and smell of manure. It was very easy to dig, indeed. His eyes widely opened in delight. From underground, he saw the carrots, the beets, the onions, and the radish, all ready to be munched on. To his joy, Meskwaki realized that he was back to the vegetable garden.

Meskwaki poked his head out of a hole. Nobody saw him. But he didn't dare to go further. He could hear the Secret Service moving and he could smell those dogs. He went back to the tunnel he had dug. And there Meskwaki napped and waited until things calmed down outside.

MEANWHILE, on the grounds of the White House, the highly trained Secret Service agents were still looking for Meskwaki. The agents seemed confused, reporting to the President about what was going on, but not exactly knowing what had set off the alarms. Jordan and Hurricane barked louder and louder as they smelled the musky scent all over the lawn, but they didn't know exactly where Meskwaki had hidden.

The two dogs had numerous talents, including being able to run as fast as a missile. Because of that, they could get to a fence-jumper in seconds. However, they were not trained for hunting, especially for hunting what they didn't see, since Meskwaki was faster than they were. Jordan and Hurricane always worked together. But Meskwaki puzzled them. One darted in one direction, the other one in another. A few seconds later, they turned around and ran towards each other. They looked around. They looked straight. They looked back. They looked left. They looked right. They looked at each other. The purposeless running disoriented them.

FROM UNDERGROUND and on the watch, Meskwaki overheard the Secret Service informing the President about what had happened. They blamed raccoons for triggering the alarms. Then everyone went back to bed, including our hero, who was so exhausted he curled up and slept for a long time in his underground chambers.

When Meskwaki poked his head out of the hole, he noticed Mr. Haney

walking the presidential dog and a few Secret Service agents around. The dog seemed thrilled to be outside. Meskwaki noticed how the dog sniffed the grounds looking for him. He also saw how the dog's initial interest suddenly disappeared when Mr. Haney threw a tennis ball for the dog to catch.

MESKWAKI, despite his sleepy eyes, never stopped watching out for any danger coming from above ground. The presidential dog's bark warned him, so he stayed vigilant. For the entire day he stayed in the underground chambers, poking his head out from one or the other exit hole whenever possible. As Meskwaki learned from his parents and other animals in the forest, only dusk and night were safe times to go out. As the night came, he felt hungry and thirsty. Like the night before, as he came out of his hole, he looked around. He flicked his ears. He sniffed the air to avoid any unexpected confrontation or surprise by the Secret Service, and especially by Jordan and Hurricane.

Meskwaki trotted to the water fountain and drank some, and then he dashed back to the Rose Garden to his hole. He was still hungry, so he peaked out again. He looked around, flicked his ears, and sniffed the air…

"Good. No dogs."

He couldn't wait for those luscious tomatoes and berries.

He darted across the lawn.

He stumbled and triggered those motion sensors.

THE SECRET SERVICE arrived. The lights at the White House went on, waking up the presidential dog, who started barking very loudly, waking up the President's entire family. By the time the Secret Service arrived at the garden, Meskwaki was already back in his dwelling without eating again.

Meskwaki had trampled the collard greens as well the beets and the carrots. From his chambers he could hear that he was in a lot of trouble now. He heard the President scolding the agents and demanding an explanation. He heard a woman's voice, the President's wife, the First Lady: "Oh, no! My precious garden! My carrots and turnips dug out, my collard greens, my lettuce tramped on, the cloches broken, torn…Enough is enough!" The First Lady had a sad and upset tone in her voice.

Her voice reminded Meskwaki fondly of Mama Bear.

From his hideout Meskwaki heard the Secret Service trying to explain to the President what had happened. Meskwaki considered that maybe this was his opportunity to deliver the letter to the President. But he was afraid of all those Secret Service agents, of the President's family, and most of all, those dogs. He was so hungry that he couldn't think clearly or make sense of things. He just wanted to be home back in the forest. He wished his parents could come and rescue him. Hiding in his dwelling, he began to whimper. No one could hear him crying.

As he cried in his foxhole, Meskwaki listened to the Secret Service agents presenting a plan to the President and the First Lady.

What little he heard, gave Meskwaki great cause for concern.

CHAPTER TEN
THE SECRET SERVICE PLAN

MESKWAKI AWOKE with renewed determination to meet the President.

He opened his crusty eyes and muttered, "It must happen today!"

At daybreak he peeped through the entrance of the hole.

"How I am going to be able to eat to gain enough strength to be able to deliver the letter to Mr. President?" Meskwaki wondered.

He needed to eat. The few grasshoppers he had been munching on had not been enough. He really wanted some of those ripe berries and tomatoes. But it seemed almost impossible to get to them.

Again he looked around and saw nobody. He flicked his ears. He sniffed the air, but this time he smelled something oddly different but also familiar to his senses.

Was that...? It was ...

Chicken!

There was something suspicious about those chunks of chicken. He hadn't seen them the day before. Meskwaki emerged from his hole and saw a carcass in what seemed like it could be a trap.

As he drew closer, Meskwaki realized the chicken was set in traps. His parents had taught him about such contraptions!

Meskwaki sniffed at the chicken. He walked around it. He tried to reach the pieces of chicken through the metal. He charmed it, just like he used to do in the forest. And finally, he pounced.

The trap went off — CLANG — scaring Meskwaki and making him jump back. He ran away from the first trap but accidentally tripped on several others, making them all to go off. He darted across the lawn. And, just like the nights before, he stumbled and triggered the motion sensors.

Soon, the Secret Service arrived. Meskwaki was long gone as usual but he heard the President saying, "Who is the most cunning of all the animals, if not a fox?"

The humans' secret plan had not worked.

The Secret Service was frustrated.

The President and his family were frustrated.

Meskwaki had escaped once again.

AND NOW, what was happening on the grounds of the White House started drawing the attention of people in town.

37

CHAPTER ELEVEN
THE MEDIA

THE FIRST PEOPLE to take notice of the new fuss about the First Lady's garden were reporters who, daily, covered the White House.

Nobody had seen Meskwaki yet, but his presence at the residence became the favorite subject of the day for newspapers and tweeters.

For the next few days there were no stories from the capital about the important social issues that the President had to deal with. There was only the news about a fox living at the White House. Not long after that, it was not only the presidential dog looking through the window glass but also TV crews, photographers, school kids, all camped outside the White House, in addition to the regular tourists who peeped through the fences of the residence in hope of seeing the new guest.

Soon, in every corner of Washington, people started tweeting or calling the news to report a fox in town, but no one ever really saw Meskwaki.

MEANWHILE, underground, Meskwaki was frustrated, weak, and sad. He started having second thoughts. He wished he wasn't the eldest in the family. He had mixed feelings about the mission, and he started missing life in the Appalachian forest, his neighbors, the forest especially, the singing of the birds, the chirp of the insects, the shade of the trees, the moonlight, the stars' lights that lit his way at dark, helping him to sneak around. He also missed the fresh, clean water from the creeks where he could swim and drink.

But it was his family that Meskwaki missed the most. He missed speaking with and listening to his family and relatives' *wow wow wow*. He remembered how he played with his siblings. He missed their playful bites, the common fights among them, the sharing and fighting for a piece of the prey that his parents brought home. He missed all the family snuggling and cuddling together on cold nights.

"What are my parents and my siblings doing now? And, dearest Mr. Raccoon, who gave me all that advice? Perhaps Mama Bear and Mrs. Great Horned Owl have forgotten about the mission. And maybe it is okay for me to return." Meskwaki thought.

BACK IN THE FOREST, the animals were also wondering about Meskwaki. Mama Bear, as usual, revealed her impatience by showing up almost every day

at the Foxes' house to ask about him. The Foxes told her that they didn't have any news about their eldest son apart from some rumor about him meeting Mr. Gray Fox and Ms. Turkey on his way to DC. The Foxes assured Mama Bear and the other animals that Meskwaki would return soon.

A fox always kept his or her word to a fox.

Meskwaki was on a mission.

CHAPTER TWELVE

MESKWAKI MEETS THE PRESIDENT

MESKWAKI FELT so discouraged about his mission and about everything that had happened so far.

Then one sunny Sunday morning, the President stepped out of the Oval Office and into the garden with a coffee mug in his hand.

Meskwaki had just peeped outside his hole.

It was now or never, he thought, so he trotted toward the President with the pouch around his neck. The bag was not in its best condition. It had become dirty and wrinkled. After all, it had been around his neck for a long time.

Meskwaki and the President looked at each other. He had never been so close to a human before. Meskwaki's heart was beating faster than usual. He paused, and the President stayed still.

Meskwaki's fur seemed redder than ever. His body seemed bigger since the time he left the forest. His semi-retractable claws were still sharp. His teeth were ready, if needed. He thought about the purpose of his journey and how he was chosen among his siblings to carry out the mission. He felt brave and feared nothing. He yapped and shook his head, trying to call the President's attention to his neck.

Addressing Meskwaki, the President said, "So, you are the trespasser? The one who has been living in my wife's garden and caused all this trouble to the Secret

Service and my family!"

The President noticed the pouch and Meskwaki bowed his head slightly so that he could untie it from around his neck.

The President cautiously reached for the bag.

He gently took the letter, opened it, and began to read:

Dear Mr. President:

We write you in light of our concerns about our environment and what our friends in the forest are facing these days. For example...

The President then read about all the animals concerns: Bernie's paw, Mr. Redheaded Woodpecker's, the Manders', Mr. Bobcat's, Flying Squirrel Jr,'s, and all the others. The letter mentioned floods, fires, and winter storms. It continued:

We suspect all these phenomena are not pure nature per se, but are caused by humans. To implement change, we understand that you, Sir, have to talk to all the people and come to a consensus, and that can be tough sometimes. However, change is needed if we are to continue our lives in the forest.

I completely understand your position and how hard it is to make everyone happy. Things in the cities are not very different from things in the forest where I govern. But we believe you are very smart and have a good heart.

Thank you, Mr. President, for your hospitality in welcoming Meskwaki to the White House.

Sincerely yours,

Mama Bear and all the animals from the forest
Transcribed by: Mrs. Great Horned Owl.

PS. Our apologies for any trouble or damage he might have caused to you and your family during his visit. He is only a boy, and he is still learning about life.

PPS: Tell Meskwaki not to worry about the Russians domesticating foxes. We had to bring it up to convince his family to deliver our letter to you.

Mama Bear's letter impressed the President.

"I assure you, my little friend Meskwaki, action will be taken to address your friends' concerns," the President said.

"Now, follow me," the President said to Meskwaki.

SO, Meskwaki followed him to the White House Press Room. Similar to the Law of the Forest, when Mama Bear called all the animals for a special meeting, Meskwaki, the presidential dog, the President's family, the Secret Service, and other humans, at least for the time being, interacted in the most natural way, without any quarrel or tension among themselves.

On that sunny Sunday, precisely at 10:30 am, the President entered the Press Room, accompanied by his family and by a little fox named Meskwaki.

CHAPTER THIRTEEN

IN THE WHITE HOUSE PRESS ROOM

MESKWAKI HELD his head high. How proud his family and friends from the forest would be now!

The Chief of Staff announced, "Ladies and gentleman, the President of the United States, accompanied by his family and..." He paused.

The President stepped forward and said, "Meskwaki, my dear friend from the Appalachian forest. Good morning, everybody!"

The President smiled, and in his typically light-hearted mood, he continued, "As you all know, for the last few days life has been different at the White House. I'd like to introduce you to Meskwaki, our guest."

Meskwaki stood still. The scene reminded him of Mama Bear standing up on the trunk of a dead tree during the council. The difference here, of course, was of all the camera flashes.

All the eyes staring at him in confusion and puzzlement!

All that attention caused him some apprehension.

The President continued, "Let's keep this short. I am sure our friend here doesn't want all this attention. I just wanted to make public the request that he brought me from his friends in the forest, and show to him my commitment as the President of the United States."

The President summarized Mama Bear's letter and appointed a special
commission to study all of the issues and take appropriate measures to improve
life in the forest.

Meskwaki felt jubilant. His eyes shined. He thought about his friends from
the forest as well as those who lived at the Zoo. He wanted to share that special
moment with all of them.

He had accomplished his mission!

CHAPTER FOURTEEN

MESKWAKI SAYS GOODBYE TO WASHINGTON

IT WAS TIME to go.

But before Meskwaki left, the President declared an hour-long state of emergency in the city of Washington, enough time to allow Meskwaki to leave the city before news of his departure spread in the media. The President didn't want Meskwaki to be bothered by the crowds that would surely have gathered to see him off. The DC Metropolitan Police and the Secret Service stopped all the cars and told all the tourists, bikers, and joggers in the National Mall to stay still.

Meskwaki, before leaving the White House, stopped by the First Lady's Garden to have a last mouthful of berries. All the traps were gone now, and he ate as much as he wanted.

Then the President walked with him to the front gate and opened it for him.

As Meskwaki left the White House, he looked up at the President with his sweet, yet sly face.

The President said, "Tell your family that I will take care of the Russians, in case you are still wondering."

Meskwaki saw something very mischievous in his expression.

They nodded to one another, as if they were now two old friends, and Meskwaki set out for the forest.

MESKWAKI PASSED by the Ellipse and crossed the Mall. He trotted down Independence Avenue and entered the Polo Field where a group of people were playing soccer. The teams stopped their game so Meskwaki could cross the field in the direction of the Potomac River, on his way home.

It would be the last time Meskwaki was seen in Washington, DC.

THE NEXT MORNING, Meskwaki's visit to the White House made it to all the newspapers' headlines in the country.

Suddenly, the story was known from New York to Los Angeles, from Miami to Des Moines, from Maine to Boise, from Baton Rouge to Juneau, from Cheyenne to Albuquerque, from Lansing to Salem, from San Juan to Honolulu, and all the other capitals. But not only people in the big cities heard about it: folks in Hollis, Oklahoma heard about it, in Good Thunder, Minnesota, in Klickitat, Washington, in Sunapee, New Hampshire, and in Bowbells, North Dakota. You name it, the whole nation heard the news about Meskwaki coming to the White House.

Of course, the story of Meskwaki's visit to Washington, DC also reached the Appalachian forest.

Some of Mr. Redheaded Woodpecker's friends overheard it, and the news traveled on their wings much faster than Meskwaki's return to the forest. Mama Bear, the Foxes, and Mrs. Great Horned Owl were happy to hear the news, but wisdom told them to wait and see, to hear from Meskwaki himself.

CHAPTER FIFTEEN

BACK IN THE FOREST

AT DAWN, a few days later, the silence of the forest was broken by a loud shout:
"MESKWAKI!!!!!" "MESKWAKI!!!!!" "MESKWAKI!!!!!"

Mama Bear had just spotted Meskwaki when she was about to call on the Foxes to ask about his whereabouts for the umpteenth time. His orangish-red fur was unique and unmistakable. She had no doubt that it was Meskwaki at the Foxes' door.

Mr. Redheaded Woodpecker, who was snacking on some grubs from an old tree when that happened, heard Mama Bear's shout, followed by a roar, once again, at him:

"Hey, Redhead! Listen to me! I need you to tell all our friends that Meskwaki has returned!"

Mr. Redheaded Woodpecker was thrilled when he heard the news and also recognized Meskwaki. Then on his swift-flying wings and the help of all his bird friends, he spread the good news. It didn't take too long for all the animals to gather to see Meskwaki. There was a chorus of joyfulness. Meskwaki didn't expect such attention. He was surprised by the Squirrel family jumping and running around him, by Mr. Raccoon hugging him, as well as with Mrs. Opossum babies, already out of her pouch, around his feet and curiously looking at him. Nor did he expect the Manders with their bulging eyes to smile at him.

All the animals from the forest came to greet him. Mama Bear and Mrs. Great Horned Owl, along with the Foxes, were euphoric.

Mama Bear and Mrs. Great Horned Owl asked about the letter and his meeting with the President. The Foxes asked about the Russians. The Foxes were delighted by how healthy he looked. Everyone was anxious to hear about his visit to Washington, DC.

Then, standing on top of the trunk of a dead tree, and surrounded by all his friends, Meskwaki recounted his adventures. Everyone was engrossed in every detail Meskwaki shared with them, from his meeting with the Gray Fox to his trip through the National Zoo to his underground bunker in a garden that smelled of roses, to the most delicious strawberries in the First Lady's garden, to meeting the President himself. Meskwaki concluded by telling his animal friends that action would be taken, that the forest would be saved.

When he finished his tale, the animals of the forest showed Meskwaki their immense gratitude for what he has done for them.

Meskwaki's voyage was recorded by Mrs. Great Horned Owl in her *encyclOWLpedia* for all future generations of animals in the forest to know.

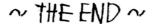

~ THE END ~

ACKNOWLEDGMENTS

THIS BOOK would not have been possible without the invaluable editing skills and the insightful suggestions by Alex Giardino. Special thanks to Rafa Antón for bringing Meskwaki to life with his illustrations throughout this edition. Thanks to Jim Block for his soccer photo and Tiago Antón for his image of Rafa. Much appreciation, to Heather Block for her beautiful layout of the book and help with its publication. Finally, thanks to José Luiz Passos, Mark Eisner, Gwen Kirkpatrick , Francisco Rogido and Steven Zausner for their unflagging support.

ABOUT THE AUTHOR

MESKWAKI AND THE PRESIDENT author Vivaldo Andrade dos Santos was born in 1964, one of 15 brothers and sisters born to illiterate parents. He grew up in a house in the interior of Brazil where there were no books, but where lots of stories were told. Vivaldo was the first in his family to attend college. His studies culminating in a PhD from UC-Berkeley. He currently is a professor of Brazilian literature at Georgetown University, and a writer of children's stories.

Meskwaki and the President is Vivaldo's second children's book, and the first to be published in English and in the United States. In 2014, while playing soccer on the National Mall on a sunny day, he spotted a red fox crossing the soccer field. It took about two years to write book, requiring research about the animals of the Appalachian forests, the White House, foxes, as well about the particular red fox who decided to live in the grounds of the White House during the government shutdown.

Vivaldo's first book, *O Rato que Roeu a Roupa do Rei/The Mouse who Munched on the King's Robe* (2009), is based on a Portuguese tongue-twister. It tells the story of a gluttonous, selfish king and a hungry mouse. The book was adopted by Brazil's national public library program and distributed all over the country. One of his favorite things to do is to visit schools in Brazil that have added the book to their curricula and talk to the students about the story, as well learn about their personal dreams. He also is involved with the Brazilian-American community where Portuguese as heritage language has been taught, and he has read his stories to the Brazilian community in Virginia, Maryland, Massachusetts, and California, in addition to Brazil.

ABOUT THE ILLUSTRATOR

RAFA ANTÓN, lives and works in São Paulo, Brazil. Originally from Vigo, Spain, he lived in Madrid and Munich, Germany, before moving to Brazil. Rafa is a self-taught illustrator of children literature and and also an author of stories

for children, including *A incrível história do homem que não sonhava* (*The incredible story of the man who wasn't able to dream*, 2014). In addition to his work in children literature, he has also worked in film production with animation, story boards, and on the creation of movie sets.

Made in the USA
Coppell, TX
29 April 2023

16193824R00038